THE GET ALONG GANG™
AND THE
TATTLE TALE

THE GET

AND THE

SCHOLASTIC INC.
New York Toronto London Auckland Sydney Tokyo

ALONG GANG™
TATTLE TALE

by **SONIA BLACK**
Illustrations by **KATHY ALLERT**

ISBN 0-590-40127-0
Copyright © 1984 by American Greetings Corp. All rights reserved. Published by Scholastic Inc.

12 11 10 9 8 7 6 5 4 3 2 1   5 6 7 8 9/8

Printed in the U.S.A.   24

The Get Along Gang,™ Montgomery "Good News" Moose,™ Dotty Dog,™ Zipper Cat,™ Woolma Lamb,™ Bingo "Bet-It-All" Beaver,™ Portia Porcupine,™ Rocco Rabbit,™ Flora Fox,™ Braker Turtle,™ and Lolly Squirrel™ are trademarks of American Greetings Corporation.

The Get Along Gang was in the school library. Dotty Dog and some of the others were finishing plans for their science projects. The school science fair was being held on Friday.

No one knew what Dotty's project would be. She said it was top secret.

Braker Turtle and Woolma Lamb were studying together. "I want to do better on this test than I did last time," Woolma told him.

"What grade did you get?" asked Braker. But Woolma wouldn't tell.

"I know. She got a *D*!" Lolly Squirrel blurted out.

"Lolly, you're such a tattletale!" Woolma said, pouting.

The gang headed straight for the lunchroom after they left the
library. Bingo "Bet-It-All" Beaver sneaked up behind Portia Porcupine.
He covered her eyes with his hands and said, "I bet you can't
guess who!"
"It's Bingo!" Lolly yelled.
"Who asked you?" grumbled Bingo.

While the gang ate, Rocco Rabbit played a trick on Flora Fox.
He took her thermos and hid it under her chair.
Flora cried, "Someone swiped my thermos!"
"I know who! I know who!" Lolly sang and pointed at Rocco.

On the way home from school, the gang stopped at the Dust Bowl for a quick game of baseball. But Dotty couldn't stay. "I have to work on my science project," she explained.

Lolly asked Dotty if she could come along to help. But Dotty said, "No. You can't keep a secret. You tell everything!"

Lolly felt awful. "Please, just give me one more chance. I won't tell. I promise," Lolly begged, and finally Dotty agreed.

Dotty's project was on the table in her workroom. "What is it?" Lolly asked.

"It's an automatic bubble-blowing machine!" Dotty replied. Lolly just stood there with her mouth wide open. "Come on," said Dotty. "We have work to do."

Lolly spent the whole afternoon with Dotty. On her way home, she met Catchum Crocodile and Leland Lizard scooping mud into a box.

"Ugh!" Lolly exclaimed. "What's that sloppy mess?"

"It's for our science project," Catchum said.

Leland nodded proudly. "We're making a worm farm!"

Lolly couldn't resist showing off. "I'm working with Dotty on her project. We follow each step that is written down in her notes. When it's done, Dotty will win First Prize."

"She will not!" Catchum answered.

"She will too!" Lolly snapped. "Dotty's automatic bubble-blowing machine will win over your stupid worm farm easily!"

"A bubble-blowing machine! That *does* sound like a winner," said Leland after Lolly left.

Catchum nodded. "But Dotty won't win with that project."

"She won't, Boss? Why not?"

"Because *we* will — with our own bubble-blowing machine."

"But how are we going to make that, Boss?" whined Leland. "And what about the worms?"

"Forget them," said Catchum shortly. "You heard Lolly say Dotty has it all written down. We'll just go and take her notes."

At nightfall, Catchum and Leland sneaked over to Dotty's. While Leland held the flashlight, Catchum reached in and grabbed the plans.

"I wish I could see Dotty Dog's face when she finds her notes missing," Catchum snickered to himself. "She'll never be able to finish her project without them."

When Dotty went to her workroom the next morning, she found the notes missing. She searched everywhere. But they were nowhere around.

"My notes!" she cried. "I can't finish my project without them!"

Dotty ran out to tell the gang about the missing notes. She was very sad. No one could believe what had happened.

"Who could be mean enough to take your notes?" Portia asked.

"Who would want them?" said Zipper.

Lolly had a guilty look on her face. "I think I know," she stammered.

Lolly told them about her meeting with Catchum and Leland.
"I didn't mean to tattle about Dotty's secret project," she confessed.
"It was an accident."
Everyone shouted angrily at Lolly except Montgomery Moose.
"Calm down!" he said. "Let's think of what we can do."

"I bet Dotty could make a new project for tomorrow," said Bingo.
"I know you can do it, Dotty," encouraged Montgomery. "We'll all help."

Dotty said she would try. Lolly promised not to say a word about the new project, so the gang agreed to let her help. Then they all rushed off to gather the things Dotty told them to get.

Dotty worked all evening on her new project. When everyone left to go to sleep, she was still hard at work.

On Friday morning the gang ran into Catchum and Leland going to the science fair. Catchum looked surprised to see that Dotty was entering anything. "May the best project win!" he said with a sly smile.

"You bet it will!" Bingo Beaver shouted back.

From the school door, Zipper and Lolly motioned
to the gang to hurry.
"Everyone has been asking about Dotty's project,"
yelled Lolly. "But I promised I'd never tell —
and I didn't."

Inside, the contestants uncovered their projects. "Catchum and Leland *did* steal my plans!" Dotty exclaimed. "That's an exact copy of my bubble-blowing machine!"

"Don't worry, Dotty," said Montgomery. "It's probably not half as good as your new project."

The judging began. Leland and Catchum started up their machine. Suddenly, a green, muddy gook gushed from the opening and splattered all over them! Everyone in the room began to laugh.

"Serves them right!" said Dotty. "They used slimy swamp water in the machine. It needs fresh water to work!"

Dotty's invention — a pedal-powered ice-cream maker — worked
perfectly for the judges. Soon real ice cream filled it to the brim.

Catchum and Leland crept away with their messy project. And the judges declared Dotty Dog First Prize winner!

"Congratulations, Dotty!" the gang cheered.

"I couldn't have done it without you, gang," Dotty replied. Then she said with a smile, "Ice cream, anyone?"